carbon dreams

violet reason

Jupines with Black Raspberries

books by violet reason
cheap visions
coyote (with Yulalona Lopez)
retreads

books from Calliope Press in 2005-2006
Musings, ed. by Crawford Washington
Masks, ed. by Crawford Washington
Night Wolves, by Yulalona Lopez
Tropomorphoses, by Yulalona Lopez
Wating for Better Times, by Conor Ciaran

carbon dreams

violet reason

calliope press
sarasota
2007

Acknowledgments
Several of these works have been published on internet
sites; several have been published in earlier versions
in earlier books. Works in the first section were assembled
from Violet Reason's notes by Yulalona Lopez.

Make-up art by Merissa dePasse & A.M. Caratheodory
Graphics by Ryan Garcia Calusa
Moscow, Idaho
ecologic@re-design.us

Publisher's Cataloging-in-Publication data
Violet Reason, 1945-2004
caebon dreams/Violet Reason
I. Title.
PS3553.A644A898 2006

ISBN 0-911385-20-7 (paper)
Manufactured in the United States of America

3 Muses Books / Calliope Press
Sarasota, Florida
editor@3musesbooks.com

Mozart and Reason Wolfe, ltd.
Wilmington, Delaware
editor@mrw-ltd.us

approximate contents

use of children
roll me again
the herd heads south
the herd rests
death in a teacup

lifeless   84
every story ends in death
seeking good death
death writes clear obits
death practices by phone
death picks up
death talks to himself
death takes a vacation
death back at work
deadlines
picnic at swan point
death the final diet
death has a crisis
death practices joking
death gets personal
death meets his match

three perspectives

"less is more" Robert Browning

"more or less" Oscar Wilde

"less is just less" babe martin

these guest writings were shared by my friend babe martin,
called by many at her own urging, 'psychobabe,' and they
chronicle her descent into homelessness. she was not only
a woman, not only once a respected doctor, but a certified,
accomplished, deeply-convicted crank allowed on the streets
only due to gross judicial incompetence. she started writing
an advice column in the globe, but after a while it appeared
dribbled in motor oil in back of Porter's store. despite
setbacks in her native boston, she continued to write the
advice column, but now it appeared scratched on hundreds of
unreadable notes kept in her sixteen plastic shopping bags, at
her new home boston alley 56 off marlborough street
(she was used to the best after all). surprisingly, she moved
relatively often for a homeless person, later living near the zoo
in portland oregon, pleased to be in warmer climes where she
wrote her column in the air by mysterious hand motions, then
in seattle, finally settling in florida to die of cancer. she was my
best friend.

violet reason

Dedicated with Deep Respect to the Memory of
    Violet Reason (1945-2004)

After receiving her MD from Columbia University, Dr. Reason
practiced medicine in Boston, an early pioneer of euthanasia
and self-mediated death (in 1975 she adopted this pen name of
Reason to protect her relatives and her colleagues, and a second pen name, Babe Martin, to give voice to a homeless friend).
Not surprisingly, her beliefs and dedication cost her her professional position, and she spent the rest of her life exploring
territories where doctors have rarely ventured. She eventually
made it to Florida, where she died homeless, but not friendless,
in July 2004.
                YL

And, dedicated fondly to the memory of Merissa DePasse
        (1945-1997)

After graduating in English from the University of Idaho, she
pursued a career in art, eventually designing books for Little
Brown in Boston, from Ansel Adams to Mad magazine. The
make-up paintings that illustrate this book (as well as other
books, including Wild Apples and Two Diaries) were produced by
her, working with her partner, Walter Cant, over a productive
and joyful 25 years. She was working on her fourth novel, when
she was killed in a crosswalk by a drunk-driving nurse.
                AMC

senseless

carbon dreams

what we dream as elements
is to match our charges
with the others
and form bonds that keep
us close and stable
through the chaos of emotion.

the angle activates
the form
as elements weave through bodies
make connections
partnerships   an even number
or a stable form.

carbon subverts the angel
of dreams by changing
electron charges. by its evenness
the images become static
perfect platonic forms
without interest or depth.

machine dreams

digital randomizations
with narrative connections from experiences
daphne from the tree, dolphine as metamorphosis
slow changes, like aging only slower, over more
than one lifetime, with machines overlapping
like mechanical metaphors.

irreverence is the modern attitude
and has the certainty of machines, based on the
neutral values of mechanical science.

rock is the base geological thingness.
words are nothing compared to holocausts
in europe, or asia, or africa, or any unknown
place or species. words are leaves next
to the inventions of technology, the weak
imitation of hardness.

what can follow science? knowledge plus value
plus ethics, as a way of living?   way?
daring exploration tempered with caution
and understanding but done peacefully
without harm to our natural matrix?
nature, the word, the idea, is abstracted
from the ground of existence.

machine city is a wasteland of abandoned—
a warehouse of unused constructs.
with vision we make order to change chaos
but vision illuminates the chaos clearly
and 'the wild sky sings'

school trap

what did school teach me? that those
who are better schooled are superior.
that those who have more money
will have a separate schooling that
will keep them separate and elite.
that knowledge is power
and power is a trap
and if you understand
then you can live in it
and be happy?
i did not learn well enough.

ambiguous service announcements

"serving the older battered woman"—
a conference on deep frying them
and how to present the meat
and what side dishes to offer

"elder abuse program"—
the official state course
on how to abuse elders
reach limits without getting caught

"meals on wheels"—
peace corps volunteers
on roller-skates serve urban cannibals
a feast in londonderry—
the skates can be reused.

academic poultry

i.
time passed indubitably
while i wrote exponentially
scribble scribble, scribble, eh,
mister dullun
for my entire reputation
not to mention my violet tenure
rested on my ability to impress
the wearers of academic dress.

the psychoanalysis of mutant values
consumed my life—
is barbarism compatible
with deformed configuration?
is speech expressive of
the capture of my singularity?
Yes! it is the vehicle of flesh
and the sculpture of love
semiotic fluxes and machine phyla
are indisputable proof
of mechanical life
polarity is bound to vanish.

the spector of housework haunts my words
with dishes, laundry, and dirt
a problem with the distribution of labor
and my own political power
who has to harness the machines
to liberate my time from—

ii.
i saw the poultry in harness
to the cold didactic muse
preparing her texts for the vortex of war—
i knew i had no excuse
and had to call incisive flames

and release the ghosts of meter

but, the poultry was hopping,
jumping from seed to seed
of every idea or justification
to continue living wild
and i could not focus my
weapons of mass destruction
i destroyed place after place
but the body count would not
increase according to projections.
recenter the ecology of human greed.

through the rear-view mirror darkly
to the light satanic mill and factory
went immaterial transformation
on the backs of mechanical dogs of war
from clay-mation to glassine vaults
light brutalism triumphant!
what is celebrated? heroic dildos?
or urban gothic swizzle
sticks in plastic sleeves?
what is the target? feminine purity?
the round is ready, pull the trigger!
penetrated by the metal gift
the body transcripts
the message. the mission
is over, rest easy.
eject the shell.

then consciousness bifurcated
and i could see above and below the cloud
standing on the heads of scholars.
i think i never should have left the house
without my rubbers, of course.
my feet were wet; it was just a dream
so i reached for the pen and thesaurus

to deconstruct and to transcribe
the essence of its metaphysical
meaning and liberate the future.

modern poultry is the attempt to overcome
silence, expounded professor pisser
silence is the shape of failure, he declared
but only silence answered him
that is, silence as the bearing
field of poultry, the proper attitude
of the living body, loud in its insistence.

when life is perverted by interference,
extinctions, holocausts, then silence
can be left behind
to invent a better reality
or rather return to silence gracefully,
gratefully, mindfully fully.

the universe of truth and beauty
is chasmic from the heterogenous ontology
of lust, because the rupture is subjective
and only the leaping genius of men
can fuse — only art can capture
the trivial forms of stature
and inform the shape of rapture
to guide the path of speech
to exceed the curse of limit—
oh, miasma, chaosmic spasms
plague our little horizons.
oh, the sadness, the waste
the car-wrecked generation of writers, the boozy
artists of cool provocation and woe
siiting in their hummers writing what they know
rapping what they dream.

bags of water

what happens when you
are floating
on the ocean,
or drinking water
on a vessel?

ts it not a bag of water
drinking water on a bag of water
on a bag of water?

skin stomach ship ocean-basin
just bags for holding water
things that keep you from combining

and losing yourself
in the whole prematurely
and maturity is everything

water is the secret
the solvent that keeps
the soul immersed
in all after bags decay.

gotta get to hell on time

gotta get there fast
doesn't matter if i die
because i'm going past
and it doesn't matter how

got to blow right by the law
and pass every single car
in sight then speed up for school
zones and drive on sidewalks

and if i crash or kill someone
i just get there sooner
give way, get out, stand aside
gotta get to hell on time

seek that warmer clime
it's all right, it's a dry heat
and that certain torture
the official loss of hope

gotta get there, gotta date
can't be slow, can't be late
don't wanna pay the price
no, no, he'll kill me twice

gotta get there fast
everyone i know is waiting
so it can't be bad
one more step, thern relax

the mathematics of homelessness

34549192 = 0

equations of equality

poetry=weakness
fame=silliness
politics=cowardice
news=catastrophe
wealth=time
happiness=wine

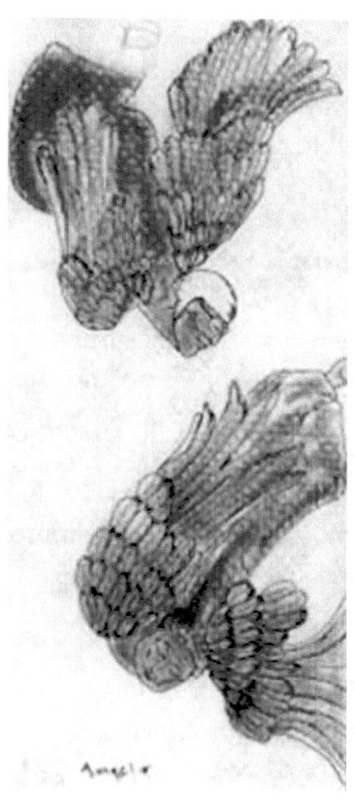

Angels

roll me

never forgot a face that paid
a dime to roll me
never forgot the dollar that rocked me
or the ten to rock and roll
on the sleeping bag on plastic bags.
not forgetting is a curse.

it is only touch i want   the faceless
gentle wrapping rapture
the backrub or caress
not the fuck
and the strained talk

i never remember the touch
and forgetting that is more than i can bear
but there is always someone
i can pay or trade for time
and if i cry i can always say
it is with indescribable pleasure

bonfire of creation

into the bonfire went his paintings   freed
from the flaws of human expression and the limits
of simple skills. the flaws disappeared
never to be seen or remembered
he watched them move to dreamtime
by degrees, by particles, the ideas now immortal,
waiting only another instance
of form in paint or gesso

too many symbols to outline a simple
idea, too many arguments for a basic
philosophy   that and its waste, paper

Paion (wherein the author calendars a charm
        for complexing comrades while cranes
        climb clouds with pedigrees)

Land is laid
The ocean is done
and I have only just arrived.

The first step is ambiguous
the second becomes ambition
and the third destination

Vestiges trace the verse.
Alternate footprints pave the halo
in miniature on colonized ground.
Weeds and their ideas grow
larger without lines.

The seeds are spread in wisps
that blind the window
and profit weeds.

The secret is not in the helix
nor in the flesh
but the living curved expression.

We fashioned a pyramid
with ourselves at the top
but we are only hybrids of ideas.

Angels without enthusiasm
are like bees without
mellilotus
                not free
but lost barren imaginings.

The brown heart
of the bear consents to a bonfire
of boughs and branches.

Astonished by green flame
the lynx is calm and watchful
in the twilight.

Raven is noisy, no
raven is noise
airsick and uncertain.

infant insults a mouse
idiot sharks an idea
Squirrel monsters disorder—
                      None speak.

Struggling to speak
to be heard amidst the
agony of many, we open.

Wine has its other uses
in the symposium of life
than to fill skeletons.

Lying in grass imbricating,
accosting each other, learning
stillness and silence.

Faust Reconsiders

Faust: "Where is the mind that conceived a world,
bore it and cherished it, joyously
released it to the air and inflated it to rival
our very spirits?"

Gadai: "The wind rustles brown leaves
in the fall, but it isn't the wind that ends
the lives of leaves, or takes the green
somewhere. it is another fuse
that we only feel but cannot see."

Faust: "With greedy hands you dig for treasure,
and are happy when you find earthworms!"

Gadai: "Exactly! The hands are in the earth
helping ideas to give birth."

Faust: "To what? To art, that is so long!?
Or to life, that is so frivolous and short?"

Gadai: "To chaos, wild chaos! The joy of destruction,
the loss of the weight of having, of memory,
lets us bloom in chaos, then be sucked
back to bloom elsewhere.
Christ, how many others have there
been, who loved woman or man,
and left them for a promise? Was it
happiness to go?

Faust: "You'll soon get bored with fields
and forests. Never envy any bird his flight."

Gadai: "Spirit's pleasure bears us both,
from volume to volume, and those
are only symbols of the life."

Faust:"I am the spirit that always denies!
A good thing, isn't it, for all that exists
deserves to be destroyed. it would have been
so much better if nothing had been created.

Gadai:"I am the spirit always denied
and I have not even lived, being obligated
to ideas and the requirements of life
and nothing, no one, has ever made me sated."

Faust:"It is so hard to contain two urges
at once, to be and to not be,
or to love nature and to master nature.
I have done it."

Gadai:"I can not, I will not. And now time
has moved on, and free of fear
and awe we choose mastery
and nonbeing. Difference is unimportant
to people today, ignorant
of the loss."

Still Life: The Artist's Dirty Clothes

Black and white stripped shirt, one arm
      over brown corduroy jeans. Black
and green chevrons on a gold velour
pullover, tangled grey trousers.   Blue
   sheets under the pile
A chef's coat stained with red paints
like a surgeon's smock covered
with blood—it was a critical operation
brown socks, blue sock holding
     empty positions
white turtleneck by the pine
dresser; blue shirt folded on a green
carpet The costumes and masks laid
       aside

    Moods attach themselves to clothes
and color their wear, after the fabric
fades from washing
               who recounts the history
of clothing, or the collapse of forms,
follows the dialectic of thread?
Only the washer.

23

Swimming at Night

Swimming out into the gulf, being lifted
and dropped by waves, slowly then looking
back, amazed at how distant
the shore has become—
have I demanded enough, too much
from myself? is there more
that I can become, by exertion
or extension? I know the land is beneath
me under the water
so what catastrophe can happen?
it is not water I fear but darkness
and if I pray often enough for light
then my life will always be like
the inside of a pearl or the wave
in front of a ray.

Circle of Murillo R.

when nothingness ceases
when needs are satisfied
when that wanes
and when awareness dims
but visions end
when self disappears
without everything
nothngness

nothingness
needs arise
there is curiosity
there is awareness
one has visions
and self is realized
one has everything
there is

The Secret of Life (Version 1283.7)

Nothingness in quantity converts itself
to being   to thingness
Stillness in quantity converts itself
To motion

Quantity to quality
sameness to difference
completeness to awareness
oneness to otherness—
Is this the secret of god
bored with oneness and completeness
desiring to be more, and, less?

Is this the secret of cancer
to be immortal like god
to convert everything to itself
and die? and be spread out?
To return to completeness and quantity
stillness and nothingness?

The game is converting, conversing
Everything converts itself into something else
Something that can be the ground
that cannot support itself anymore
much less the lightest thought or theory
and conversion is a trap,
once converted it cannot go back
but you can remember
and converse about it.

No, it can convert, and does.
it reverts to its previous state
but the pattern moves on
and the pattern can move without the matter
in its form in its particularity
like a blue guitar or palm tree in the mind

Hydrogen converts itself to helium, iron
to actinium, single elements to molecules,
molecules to enzymes,
and only great force can revert them.

Enzymes to organs
accidents to reproduction, single cells to many,
single levels to embedded levels, planes to folds
and lines to active coils, and it continues,
duplication to sex.

And hydrogen converts its home, reducing to oxidizing,
sea to land, land to air, fins to hands,
cartilage to spines, jelly to skin,
skin to carapace or feathers
spewing and spawning to internal eggs
carriages to cars, coal to fusion,
finger counting to computers

People convert forests to grasslands, and grasslands
to fields of wheat and those to dust, and dust
to concrete and lung disease. The final conversion
is not always what we intended.
Weeds convert bare ground into a paradise
of weeds, but the work of weeds,
the shade of weeds, the mold
and litter of weeds
provides the homes for flowers and trees
that crowd out weeds
who have to bank their seeds
and wait for the next conversion back to bare ground.

Rock is converted to pyramids, people
are converted to pyramids
of power and value, animals and algae to parts
of the pyramids. The pyramids become inverted
and animals become more valuable, and weeds

and bacteria become most valuable.
What is value but what is wanted? Dung
is more valuable than gold
to a beetle who converts it to
the flesh of beetles.

Converted, reverted, perverted,
change moves through traps remaking
the traps from the flesh of the trapped.
And value inverts so what is needed
is desired more than what is rare
but you know that.

homeless

stages of defeat

you keep working, but are dominated by your tragedy;
you lose interest in eating or sleeping. you clean your home,
though, still thinking about the event, and rehearsing
your reactions over and over and over.

you sleep with the aid of pills. you eat quite a bit, but only
good, sweet foods, because this is the only good thing
in your life at this time. you go to work but leave early
for appointments. mid-day amusements, such as bowling
or drinking, rank high.

you are annoyed by the good attentions (or neglect)
of your friends and family. you cannot be reached. you sleep
much more; work becomes an unpleasant memory. alcohol
or other chemical modifiers retain their fascination.

useless things, such as furniture, coin collections, leather
shoes, or appliances, seem to trickle away from you, like
urine down a sidewalk. you get angry when your musings
get interrupted. you retreat to your cardboard-covered
piece of sidewalk.

you are amused by the preoccupations of others,
the time-driven, money-oriented, thing-obsessed many.
you notice birds, rodents, flowers, and weeds. you get
more exercise and have a more balanced diet,
depending on the dumpster route. you are free.

life goes on, does it?

"waddaya wan?" she asked.
                          "my friends they told me life
must go on," he said.
                          "oh, a patient," she pursed her lips
and nodded, "have a seat over here, on this can.
my fee is twenty-five cents, or a bottle," she stared

at the brick wall, forgetting the bottle for a moment,
her voice, now, as soothing as any medicine:
"they said life must go on? why? where's it going?
tell me your story, the whole thing, chronologically."

he did, while she poked at a pile of rags with a stick.
"you lost everything," she agreed, "your wife, your home,
children, investments, retirement, car, job—your clothes
are nice, you still have those." he fingered his sleeve.

"you could start over, going back to school or getting
a new job, save for another twenty-five years, buy
new things, find a woman, start a family—but there
is no rule that it all cannot be taken away again.

"if i were you, i'd go for society's throat, start selling
guns to children, try writing crucial messages
on walls, drop out of the system, off the grid, subvert
people with radical ideas, move to cambridge.
"life goes on, things get better, life is good—ha! myths,
just myths to enslave you. you could stop, just do
nothing, not work or eat—protest, make a statement,
or stay here with me, i could teach you—"

mean of life

ed, a young bearded homeless man in camouflage
clothing and sneakers asked, "is this it? this
is it? everything? where is there any meaning?"
  "do you expect meaning?" she answered, straightening
the newspapers over her sore-covered legs finding
a crumb of godiva chocolate (she was used
to the best after all) on page seven.

"yes, i do," he said, "otherwise why bother?"
                      "why bother what?" she replied, "living?
eating, sleeping? have you seen the alternative?
a plastic box in pile of dirt near a church?"
she reached and moved a greasy lock of hair
from his nose. "listen, you don't have to be here,
you could go house to house asking for work,
others have gotten lucky, it just takes one break."

she poked one of her less certain molars and continued,
"the meaning here is simple, through a combination
of bad choice, bad luck, bad economics, and a society
that cherishes selfish entertainment, you have
been sorted from the comforts of rewards to the light
disposal area tolerated on the fringes. there is plenty
here, it's not like india for christsakes, look at your
sleeping bag—it's waterproof. your nikes, your whatever—

"you know for months i slept in the cab of a rusty reo truck
until it was taken over by railhead red—did i complain?
no, because it is not the fitter who survive but the most
cooperative. life is not won by people with the most
money, but enjoyed by those who are most open to
the freshness of an october leaf, like this one,"
she traced its veins under a scarlet blaze. "this
doesn't mean anything, it just is. we just are,
everything just is and continues until it does not.

never mind, i sound like a soundbite for death.
could you get me a drink of water, please?"

f-art

espied i it on my way to the university dumpsters.
it hunkered into the pavement by the student union,
as if embarrassed by its own lack of symmetry
or meaning, a misshapen blob of metal and dirt,
unrelated to its surroundings, disconnected
from any theoretical or autistic i mean artistic
foundation. there are those who criticize this kind of art,
saying that the artist exercised no vision and little
discipline, other than signing it and pocketing
the fee. not only will i defend such art, but i urge
the expansion of the category to include my own
contribution to art, 'found art,' f-art in short.
for example, later that same day, i saw a perfect
example of an organic torroidal concretion left
on the sidewalk, unique in its textural composition,
and forceful in its ontological presence. delicate
in its compositional harmony. discrete in its colors—
so many shades of brown and grey—
engagingly multidimensional, it was a veritable
metaphor of the complexity and brevity
of life, a celebration of the joy of eating and excreting.
it was shit. true, shit. but art is coprophilous as well
as abstractly symbolic. and this expression
was as evocative as the pile of metal and dirt seen
in the morning. can we not all recognize
the art in everything, and respect it?
careful, though, not to step in it?

ravenna freedom

"i don' understand. the streets aren't freedom?"

"it used to be that being disconnected, from organizations,
companies, or churches, meant freedom. now it means
having no money, no home, nothing anyone wants. oh, yes,
i am still free, but freedom has lost a lot of meaning.
i would prefer to be free to have a garden, to build
something a little better than this cardboard, tin
and carpet coat castle that you see.

"that was what wilderness used to mean you know.
it was the symbol for freedom. you could be free
in the forest, free to hunt, and explore. now, i am here
in seattle and i am free to walk from second street
south and then under the freeway and up the hill,
as long as i come back, and am not discovered
underneath the ravenna bridge, oh merde.

"the system shall eat you up and spit you out,
then blame you for being eaten and excoriated
into a little piece of crap wrapped in someone
else's throwaway clothes."
"you survive."

"i am not surviving. oh, the first time i lost
my job at the hospital—i was a doctor
you know—i laughed about it. the triumph
of petty bureaucrats over the independent
thinker concerned with granting a good
death to people in indescribable pain. then
later, i lost my job as grade school nurse.
that was a death sentence. i had nowhere
to go. after a time, money flowed away
and suddenly i had no place, no friends
who could give me another night on
the couch; no cash, no handouts. i became

what you see now. my fall was more dramatic
than most, but i understood what was happening
better than most. and, now i cope better
than most but i remember locked doors
and sleeping through whole nights, i remember ..."

"hey, wanna get warm?"

xxx-mas

"this is it? this is it? the gift of the seasons?"
she hurled the old sock away.
"no, thank you, i have everything that i was given at the start,
eyes to see, lungs to breathe, all the equipment
to live and meditate. this crap that people
have to have, it is that, crap,
and that is what is pornographic,
not people intersecting their various curves in photographs,
but the lust to have more things than
you can carry, more than you can even see at once,
more than you ever need,
more than you have time to appreciate or care—
you know, time is the greatest gift to be given,
and that is all you really have to give that is your own.
and that is all i want, just some more time,
to lie under the cedar in the rain ...
ahh, to rest ... and see ..."

alley angels

"have you ever seen angels?" he asked.

"you mean fat bald white men with 900-dollar
shoes handing out twenty dollar bills?
yes, once," she sighed.

"no, i mean beautiful romance book
hunks and babes comforting the sick
so they don't go postal and make more
people miserable—well, maybe fat black
women blessed with the wisdom of poverty,
well, you know what i mean."

"no, no, i prefer quakers to angels. they can feel."

"would you like to see, feel an angel?"

"feel an angel's soft breath, fetid with methane
like any hungry cow. no. why?"

"but they are real, we must praise them!"

"sure, yeh, hail divas of earth and sky, pour
your healing fluid on our poor lives,
come to our aid and guard our meager
lives and be with the blessed children and elders."

"amen, woman."
                    "but can they give us soup"
"are you bitter?"
                    "don't know, never ate my own flesh,
not that desperate yet"
                            "are you sour?"
"get off my coat, and be glad that
we are free to breathe and fly
like any startled pigeon."

origins

"stop looking at me! just take a picture and eat it. well?"
"i know you"
                    "not in a biblical sense i hope"
"no, from the library. i looked you up on the internet"
"it may have been a mistake to show you the library—
libraries are for sleeping, not tracing."
                                    "i couldn't help it,
you are fascinating."
                    "only in abstraction. i shit my pants
this morning."
            "as normal as breathing."
                                "will you clean it up
for me?"
        "if you can't."
                        "never mind. what travesty did
the internet show, what did you find?"
    "you were a doctor, you helped people achieve a good
death."
        "you understand?"
                        "you kevorkianized them"
"you don't understand."
                        "you gave them a choice, the power
to choose, the strength to choose."
                            "you do understand,
maybe. now what?"
            "tell me why?"
                            "are you one of us?"
                                            "us?"
"the really homeless or are you a reporter? one of them?"
"them?"
        "the entertainment predators? the users?"
he fingered his beard, combing it with his nails: "no, just
a seeker of knowledge."
                    "knowledge or curiosities?"
"things, facts, science, myths, stories ..."

"everything, everyone has a story," she smiled,
probing a weak tooth.

"i know," he said, "and it would take
a lifetime to tell it," he pontificated.

"don't be silly,"
she said, "most of life is habit and repetition. no biography
should be over a hundred pages long. it simply
isn't interesting to hear about the thousandth
clinical fuck or millionth beery binge"

"or the tenth patient?"
"or the second patient, dammit. people want, need
a private death, like any road kill cat."

"how did you get
here?"

"i offended the medical profession. i took my oath
too seriously, have you ever read that oath?"
"no."

"read it first."

"tell me first."

"pledge, help, no harm …
of course so much is unsaid and left to interpretation.
it should be rewritten for modern body mechanics."

she pulled at her underwear: "we should discuss this later,
after our ablutions."

"can sweet words make messy functions
sound elegant?"

"fuck off and get me a newspaper."
"here," he pulled one from his bed, "would you tell
me how you got here?"

"thanks," she tore off a piece of paper
and wiped inside her pants. he watched without commenting,
but scratched his neck, thinking a flea, another carnivore.

"here in sarasota," she started, "it's so much warmer
than on marlborough street, and i do believe i've found
the fountain of aging, or at least it would seem so to those
who do not drink from it. you're too young to be homeless."

"there are many younger."

"but, unless you like it,
the young can always get jobs or sponsors."
"you mean pimps?"
"no, sometimes just people who help."
"you mean angels."
"don't test me. why are you here?"
"i offended the legal profession."
"is that possible?" she gasped
dramatically, "what, you denigrated forty percent fees?"
"no, an ignorant judge, who let a ward of the court suffer,
i, well, i … i left under bad circumstances, owing time
and money to that same court."
"good for you, dear, now let's try
the dumpster on 14th, i'm sure the story can wait."
he smiled and shrugged; it wasn't going to be as easy
as he'd thought.
she thought that if she ever read anything
about herself in that yellow paper, this guy was going
to have to be sent to sleep with the manatees.

roll me again

never forgot a face that paid a dime to roll me
never forgot the dollar that rocked me or ten to rock
and roll on the plastic bags on the hillside.
it is only touch i want the faceless gentle wrapping
rapture, the soothing backrub or light caress
not the fuck and strained talk.

i never remember the touch and forgetting is more
than i can bear but there is always someone
i can trade for time and if i cry i can always
say it is from indescribable pleasure.

tao of home

"welcome home, babe!"
                    "home, what home?"
                                        "sorry.
what's this?"
                    "sleeping bag, not a home not a place."
"what about those people, us?" he asked, gesturing.
                    "we homeless are becoming so many
and so many more are becoming homeless
not because we cannot find or keep our homes
but because the homes are being destroyed
the whole mother f-ing frame for homes is falling apart
not just for people but for mammals and frogs and other
beings. not bacteria though or viruses or molds
or rats or cockroaches—we are making more homes
for them each time we try to destroy them with chemicals
and poisons, medicines and cures, we offer them more
opportunities, more places for them and strengthen
their holds on those places but we could not live
in those homes—"
                    "so?" larry asked, "they live with us."
    "so i guess we are making more homes with a net gain
and that is very taoistic that the lowest shall flourish
and the largest and richest shall fail and disappear.
poetic justice is better than no justice at all. at least
there shall be a universe of bacteria, amoeba and cells
if wolves, frogs, and humans cannot make it."
                                        "ouch,
scrolled ideas way too heavy for a soggy cardboard
universe."

use of children

"you have children?" ted asked, picking his nose
and flicking the result onto the sidewalk.
      "is there a reason you're asking, professional or
personal?" babe asked.
            "jesus, you're suspicious,"
ted stood up.
        she nodded.
            "alright, i was thinking
of my daughter. hadn't heard from her in a while."
      "why wouldn't you live with her?"
               "she's useless."
"all children are useless, we push them out and force
them to behave our way. then our children push us out
and away, and we pull them out and in. then
they antidote our doting on the tired environment
by burning it. and we all warm ourselves by the flames
and plant seeds in the ashes."
           "what? but i worry
about her."
      "and i worry about him. i tried to get him
to lighten his load."
        "who? who is him?"
            "never mind,
you never met him. i put his paintings into the bonfire,
freed them from the flaws of media expression
and limits of simple skills. the flaws disappeared
never to be seen or remembered; i watched them move
to dreamtime by degrees, by particles the ideas
now immortal, waiting only another instance of form
in paint or gesso."
        "what a waste," ted said, spitting
over to the gutter, "whose child are you?"
    "doesn't matter, hold me,"
           "hold me, roll me, kiss—"
"shut up," she said, leaning over.

the herd heads south

like that movie, urban cowboy, the sick and tired moved
south by bus to a new world of play and warmth.
and a new beginning. why did i go? she thought, i'm dying
of cancer as my body is subverted by immortal cells
that do not concern themselves with the welfare
of their host, a benign disease that does not offend
with pustules or flying mucus, just the slow decay
of bones as tumors replace the bone. i cannot fall again,
that is all. i cannot get sick, and cannot host a cold.

her first visit was to a grocery store. a new chain to her,
called publix, pubics she called it, but built on the same model
of a fluorescent heaven, displaying the cornucopia of food
and drugs. she was able to sample many of the foods
discretely. it was made easier by the fact that some old
people were stationed at tables by the end of every aisle
giving out samples of pizza, fish, and crackers.

she was speaking to her neighbor, 'tommy flash,'
"had trouble crossing the street, these drivers
they do not care and do not look unless they take aim."
        "next time, take an empty grocery cart with you;
the drivers cannot risk damage to their hummers or toyotas."
        "good idea, then i can turn it over and sleep under it."
"do you have a place? no? it is summer now, so the getting
is good. why, you ask? the snow-bird bums have moved
north for richer panhandling circuits. here, let me show
you a good place. 'soldier bob' left last month. he was living
behind those condos, by the fence. you can only be seen
from a small path there by the stream, oh, or by
an alert shopper at bealls, but they rarely look that far.
oh, and you will need a spot to sit. soldier bob used
to sit by the exit near the publix, but it was hard
for cars to stop there. i'd suggest that curve by
the pond—people can see you in advance and pull
out of traffic to hand you a dollar. you have an advantage,

being a woman and all; there are few of you and you
get more concern, if you play it. me? no problem.
i have my places further down the tamiami trail,
near the college. students are well off and generous, when
being homeless is thought to be a romantic career move."

the herd rests

she took his advice. nevertheless she was surprised
when he visited her a week later, with a proposal.
"let's take a trip to dizzeyworld with animal ed. he's got
a car for the day. it's only a two-hour drive to dizneyworld."
        she sputtered: "dizneyworld? epcot center?"
"hey, i never heard of apricot, what is that?"
        "never mind. how do we get in?"
                                        "tickets, left over
from graduation; i got six. you know anyone else wants
to go?"
        she shook her head, at a loss for words.

the ride was at high speed, although not as fast
as the south-bound bus had been. she watched
the landscape flow by, wondering what would it
be like to run this fast? a new race of people
who needed speed and could not bear to move
slowly or to give slow things their attention.

at the edge of the parking lot she paused. her friends
stopped too, but looked into the gates, eager to taste
the treats. she started walking again, more slowly,
letting herself be dragged by the guys. all she
remembered of that day was lines, punctuated
by brief action rides, then more lines before food.
of course, they also checked out the trash cans,
even found a ten-dollar bill wedged against a fence.
she decided to find a place to rest.

when she was sitting in the shade a coyote stopped
in front of her. she spoke to him, recognizing
the trickster inside—no normal coyote would be
so calm and composed in human crowds. he was
a handsome brown, except for a spot of mange
near the tail. she invited him to stay in the shade
with her, but said that the blanket was clean
and hers. she looked into his eyes, sure that she
had offended him with her prim possession
of the blanket, but the look in his eyes faded
suddenly and he burped, sending a toxic scent
of gases her direction. she could smell old hot dogs
and popcorn. she automatically said, " take
some ginger for that, or else baking soda." the look
of intelligence and mischief returned to his eyes;
   he thought perhaps she might be a colleague of doctor
vulture, but she was not made-up, groomed
or dressed for professional success; he smelled urine
and her body odors. he licked some grass
from her knee, then trotted out into the crowds,
looking for his family.
                         she lay down on her blanket
and waited for the men to return from their trip
to the rest room to take showers. then
she could get cleaned up.

death in a teacup

later that same memorable day she saw the face
of death riding in a teacup, with a strange smile.
she waited for him until the ride had ended
and spoke, "how can i see you? are you real?
am i getting ready to die?"
                       —surprised, he answered,
"you have been acquainted with death before.
i am just the face of the process, makes it easier."
      she spread her hands but said nothing. he said,

43

"in time, but your bones have reached a plateau
that could extend for years. just keep your immune
system healthy. more fruits and vegetables, vitamins,
extracts and enzymes. you'll be fine." he touched
her hand. she was not able to se his eyes very well.

she asked him more questions and he answered them.
she asked questions about her friends, about life
and death, and meaning—
                     it was so hard to remember
meaning when all there was around you was sun,
money, palms, and fun. every uncertainty
and unpleasantness had been pushed out of sight
and beyond the edge of consciousness, so this seemed
like normalcy, waiting for rides, eating, anticipating
another day of hurrying and resting. she could not wait
to get back to her palm by the fence and contemplate
everything. she had expected to see giant mice and fat
pleasant burghers enjoying them, not a mythical
trickster or the face of death. she ran her fingers
through her hair, traced her breasts, rubbed her thighs,
relishing the feeling of being alive,
                        homeless, but free.

lifeless

every story ends in death

you held his head while he vomited
thinking it could only get better
but knowing that you could never
see that white woolen carpet again
without the ghostly yellow stain.

you rubbed her head until she slept
looking up at the textured off-white
ceiling as your future together unfolded
as a series of happy vignettes where
each success was surpassed by another.

you nursed him after the crash
then through the cancer treatments
and finally after the stroke that took
his whole identity. now, nothing
was left but the tenacity of life
sticking to the beating heart.

after making love sublimely, she said:
"i'm too fat, and old, my skin
is loose," and she pushed her ears back
and looked in the mirror and nodded.
and you could see the future stretch
out as well, even though you loved her.

you each vowed that you would stay
together, in love, regardless of flaws
and errors of judgment, regardless of fate
and all the permutations of time thrown
in your way, and you almost made it—

but every story ends in death, in bed
on soft grey and yellow striped sheets
or on the concrete illuminated by a few
hard lights, under strangers' gazes, who
think that their story will be different.

seeking good death

joe got off work and came home
careful to take off the greasy coveralls
with his name stitched on the pocket.
he relaxed in his favorite chair and
when pearl came to get him for dinner
she could not waken him from sleep.

bette lost her grip on the cliff edge
falling is easy, she thought
then looked at the clouds above
her until they disappeared.

paul reached for the slab of wood
then knew he shouldn't have, his hand
was gone before he could shout
to stop the saw. after the blood
slowed, he composed himself.

darlene slipped as she crossed the stream
fell and hit her head. the current took
her corpse then played with it, lifting
the arm, turning the head, before
depositing it onto sand to rest.

cycling down the mountain, alan saw
the crack before it launched him
into the rocks—he bounced
and bounced until he successfully
rolled to the canyon floor.

the grizzly crushed jim's skull, sniffed
the remains and ambled away.
small worms explored still passages
until the tunnels collapsed.

when ann stopped swimming, she sank;
the arms floated to embrace,
then fish distributed the gift
among the levels of the sea.

hannah lay in the grass, watching flowers
until no breath disturbed their petals.

death writes real obituaries

tiffany drove too fast through
a red light because rafe, the bastard,
hit her for the thirtieth time, so
she wanted to escape. three others
died in the accident, but doubtless
they were just as unhappy.

albert collapsed, after eating a cake.
from stress and depression, he had turned
to sugar and fats—oddly enough
the president of the bakery died
the same day from complications
of fat-clogged arteries from overeating.

after learning he had cancer, sam
followed the directions of those who
treated the symptoms of the problem;
he kept eating what he wanted and drinking
and overworking without enough sleep
until the treatment and his life killed them both.

death practices by phone

hello, my name is death—what? death, yes,
no, i know your name. no, it's just a survey.
if you were to die this moment. well, no,
i was considering giving everyone a brief advance
notice, time for one last statement—yes,
a prayer, yes. i'll come back later for—

okay, you're a lawyer; sure
you can make a plea but you
won't be able to afford the cost.
i don't know; hell, i'd guess.

i understand you are a doctor
but in this situation, you're on earth
and it's nothing that death can't cure.
no, i don't think that it's absurd.

what do i believe, as death?
that you should make the place
a little better, not by trying, but
just by living well, consciously.
and now i believe it is your time.

what? sorry mom, misdialed.
yes, okay, i'll wear them, yes,
love you, yes, said, love you!
by the way, how are you feeling?

who called me coyote?
i can find out where you are.
don't like that at all
you cannot hide forever.

no, not like that, think
of it as the perfect diet
the purity of bones

unencumbered by muscle or fat
(which only the living need),
organs, skin, connective tissue—
well, you are no longer connected.

"death! how interesting!"
    "i know, i only personify dissolution,
but it works! you know, you understand
how lives are diced on time's noisy
chopping board—you know that echoes
last longer than the brief cries of existence."
    "so, death is silence?"
        "no, no, noise is existence
from the cries of pain to the popping
and snapping of quantum foam, unheard
of course by beings with ears."
    "death isn't funny!"
        "why not?
the alternative is boring and serious."

death picks up

i am the angel of death.
    no it really makes no difference
    you will not be remembered
    even as a myth, for it is not you
    that's remembered anyway,
    just a pattern of what others think
    they saw. come now

i am the angel of death
    what is your request?
    you have only seconds left
    be careful what you choose

"what about my soul?"
        "your soul died years ago."

"what! how i can i die without one, an immortal
soul, i thought ..."

        "it is easy to die. just become
nothingness, like the bubble after it pops."

    "but, that's ridiculous how could my soul die first?"
"it started with the first lie and accelerated
with each false action and accusation, each wayward
step, every insult ... you see?"

        "but, my soul is immortal!"
"no, just a myth. each soul forms after consciousness,
flowering slowly but more delicately than the brain
or body, than feeling or emotion. it is—"

        "that's shit!
i demand a hearing, a judge!"

        "of course, i am patient,
as patient as you. i always listen—"

        "no, someone else.
your boss. god!"

        "sorry, there is a partner,
but we never overrule one another. you have
to make the case with me ... or be silent."

    "no, the soul is like a star, goethe said it shines
unceasingly—"

        "goethe was very smart, but look
at the night sky; what do you see?"

        "stars, billions
of stars."

        "very good, but you cannot see the trillions
of invisible dead stars. in deep time, even stars,
like souls, stop shining."

        "oh."

"yes, you are facing death at last
put down that spray can, defacing death
is not allowed, nice letter though,
this cloth absorbs so much. now
just release your hold ..."

death talks to himself

"no one understands. the tree of life
is the tree of death. you ascend as you
grow then you descend. the tree is one
giant exchange with the living and non.
the tree is, i am, all else is, or is not."

"death is not someone or something you know—
there is only a flow of holons in patterns
or the cultural, conscious, beating heart,
the resting corpse, the decaying statue, and finally
the forgotten words, all of which dissolve
through flowing time, as more are formed
and replace them and fade away themselves."

"yes, i know, it's old. i suppose i need a riding mower
now that the scythe has gotten rusty, except for africa
hmm, i'll have to keep it and clean it for a while longer
i guess. for europe a miata. and for the pacific region
a regatta ... but what should i get for california?
a hog, a beamer, a volvo wagon?"

death takes a vacation

death parked his hummer in a handicapped space near
the entrance to dizneyworld; perhaps he would help
a few souls, then enjoy the rides and confusion of people
trying to be happy. but, the first thing he saw on the way in
was a coyote. strange to see him not skulking in the bushes,
but strolling like any tired visitor or weary canine family
member. not just any coyote then, but the mythic
being who had stolen the sun. he touched the radiation
poisoning on the tail as he walked past, taking the last
of that energy and those crazy cells. coyote flinched
and looked up but did not growl or run,

                                                "i am sort
of a trickster myself," said death.

                                   coyote snuffed, still
disappointed by his treatment in the cathedral of the mouse,
but when he felt a cold shiver and looked around, the man
was gone. his tail did not itch.

on the way to the first ride, he saw someone to bless,
a blubbery guy named cam, whose overindulgence finally
was going to pay off: "i am death, i see you are in distress,
and you know there is nothing left."

                                   "i, uh, did not expect
a person, just numbness and then darkness . . . my heart?"

      "yes, not enough exercise, the veins dried up. touch
my hand."

            "okay, now what?"

                              "no argument, no last prayers?"
death was surprised.

                  "no, i did this to myself. i could
have fasted and died later, but i chose the path of pleasure.
i could have shot ... where are we?"

                                    "still here, just not visible
to anyone."

            "what am i now, then?"

                              "you are the echo

of your consciousness, you will fade into the vibrancy
of all being, adding your echo to the patterns of sound in trees
and the flesh of weeds, to all living flesh."

"then, there is nothing
after life?"

"no, there is everything, but you must disperse
completely to participate in everything, you see, it is lighter
now, you can see fewer details, fewer edges, good bye now."

"yes, yes."

after his next ride, the swirling teacups, he noticed
a woman watching him, a thin prim woman with a patrician
expression that he recognized from boston, or maybe
marblehead; her clothes had once been good. he walked
to her. she introduced herself and asked if she was going
to die. he assured her that she would live a while longer.
she said that she once was a doctor. he replied
that maybe she could have more than one purpose in living.

"what is it to die? she asked."

"you know, it is simply to cease
to breathe, for the heart to cease to beat, to cease to live.
it is the collapse of one level of complexity to a simpler
level. the you that is you disperses, leaving only organs
and cells that are no longer organized, then they collapse
and are prey to bacteria, viruses, sharks, coyotes, all
the things that break you down to pay off your debt—"

"debt?"

"debt to nature, for all the lives that you took
so you could live, the lives you destroyed by accident,
or the ones you interfered with—"

"okay, okay,
i got the idea. somehow i thought you would be terse,
a grim silent reaper of souls."

"no, i always talk to people,
especially the ones who are afraid or the ones who want
to know more."

"what are you, exactly? the king of death?

the angel of death?"

"i prefer angel, but i am more like
a spirit outside of the normal dimensions of time."

"are you an angel like lucifer or gabriel?"

"no, i am not
related to any one religion or belief. i am more universal.
i adhere to any being that is dying and observe and participate
in the process."

"i don't understand."

"and i can not explain
it any better than i can explain the reason for and expression
of eleven dimensions in my universe."

"don't you ever want to interfere in the process?"

"of course,
and i do. some people are really not dying; some can be
helped with a kind word or touch. a few need a push away so
they do not ruin so many others lives—"

"aren't you worried
that you will alter the order of the universe?"

"no, the order
of the universe is what we all make it, what we all contribute.
without the ability and power to choose, there would be much
less reason to live, don't you think?"

"yes, i am glad
that you confirm my feelings about choosing and changing
things. thank you for your time. are you here for a reason?"

"of course, vacation, to rest and look around, but i may
do a little work while i am here. there is always something
that cannot wait, you know?"

"yes, have fun."

"thank you,"
death replied, "and you also. feel the breeze?"

after a few more silly rides, through darkness with large
scary figures or space themes, death went outside. he stopped
by a teen-aged boy in back of one of the stands, saying:
"i am the angel of death, i will wait until you need me.

do not worry, do not move." the boy's mouth moved
but no sounds issued; he was clearly frustrated that
he could make nothing happen, not sounds or movement.
death cradled his head and watched the small bubbles form
at the corner of his mouth. when the confusion left
the boy's eyes, death showed him how he would change,
how it was good and how it would benefit the cycle of life.

it was not a long day, although it was more interesting
than most. he reached into his pocket and took out a folder
that he found in the gift shop. it was for the holland
america line, for a cruise on the ship veendam. perhaps
a cruise would be relaxing. the people might be older
and more receptive to his messages. he smiled.

"i am death. come with me to shed
this mortal coil and to join the eternal flow
that you call heaven. come now, release your hold
and enter the—"   what was he doing, practicing again?
he was on vacation.

death at work

applicant #4,300,3448.433
death: what?

　　mr. 433: my soul, what about my soul?
d: your soul is, i mean was, a delicate thing,
assembled by your sensitivity to others, and through
your attachment to a place. what was your place, exactly?"

　　mr. 433: Umm, well, i don't know, miami, i guess.
d: miami? is that a real place now? i suppose. but, let's look
at your history here: detroit, portland, wilmington, buffalo,
la, chicago, miami. were you ever anchored somewhere?
probably not, you don't have a soul left. it was spread so thin
it evaporated with your travels. that happens.

　　mr. 433: But, what will happen when i die?
d: nothing, i expect. nothing at all.

applicant #4,398,038,001
　　ms. 001: i know, i know. don't i get a second chance?
death: no.

　　ms. 001: why not?
d. well, you had seconds, thirds, fourths. you have had
74 years, two months, two weeks and three days of life.
that's over 27,000 days, over 650,000 hours,
300 million breathes, almost 3 billion heartbeats. wow!
did you think you had to go straight in line towards
one goal? money?

　　ms. 001: not fair. i didn't just want money. i wanted
happiness, comfort, maybe a little fame.
d: and were you alone in this universe?

　　ms. 001: of course not. i had a family. i—i want a second
chance. i deserve a chance to make things right
d: they are right. or wrong. or it doesn't matter, the balance
is of the whole, not you. wait a minute, my cell phone is
vibrating.

　　　　hello, yes. yes, i was with 4,398,038,001.
sure, we were discussing her—oh for christ's sake. Yes
i know, 'your' sake, then. but, i don't like being called

on particulars. maybe we can trade. can i have falwell,
now? he's at the end of his usefulness. seriously,
look at the man. how much lower could he—oh, alright.
okay. we'll talk soon."

                        turning to the overweight real estate
agent, death said: "i'm not going to call it a second chance,
let's call it a preview, with the option to sell. get out of here.
and be good." he looked at his running shoes and muttered,
"damned do-gooder."

applicant #4,411,219,954
    mrs. 954: "i'm on the toilet, go away!"
death stood silently.
    mrs. 954: "can i see some id please?"
death showed her his fingertips.
    mrs. 954: "someone will see me. i didn't agree to this!"
d: "ah, yes, it's in the contract of life. death is part
of living, the last wonderful part in fact. where there is no
living there is no death—would you want to be a statue,
lifeless and buried?"
    mrs. 954: "yes, if it meant no decay!"
d: "but you would not be living or aware—time carries
its own annihilation."
    mrs. 954: "come now, i have years to go, my doctor has
negotiated with the disease and i should live another year."
d: "the negotiations broke down it seems, now come with me."
    mrs. 954: "no, it is not my time. it is not right or fair!"
d: "how can you argue?"
    mrs. 954: "medicine has progressed, luxury has progressed
but not our ways of dying!"
d: "no the ways of dying have progressed, the chemical
automotive, nuclear—"
    mrs. 954: "no, i mean you, the way of death"
d: "perhaps some things cannot be improved."
    mrs. 954: "the horror is the time counting down, until only
years or seconds are left."
d: "you have that backwards; time is being added
to your life, until it extends—"

mrs. 954: "it's the aimlessness, the unknown uncertainty
i cannot stand. the fear of death, the fear of the words tagging
death, dying, departing, like some ugly taboo that one
cannot help but violate."
d: "here is complete certainty, nothing to fear."

applicant #5,000,000,000

mr. 000: "take one the them, not me, the true one!"
death: "the fundamental truth is that we all die, we have to die
for renewal to happen."

mr. 000: "what is the goal of life? rightness, no, i meaning, i
mean—that is, no!"
d: "a set of unique instants, never to be repeated, in
the history of the universe, makes your life unique
and meaningful."

mr. 000: "what do i get?"
d: "the experience."

mr. 000: "nothing more?"
d: "that is a true and precious treasure, now go."

deadlines

"will you sleep with me?" sheila asked death, who coughed
and said "no, i never sleep."

"no, you know, i mean have sex?"
death sighed, thinking what was the attraction for some?
forbidden vapors? most were repelled and avoided looking
at death directly, "no, it would not be, ah, fitting."

"literally?" she asked, touching his arm; she was interested
and had more questions: "are you the death of everything
living? how would you take an otter's soul?"

"death becomes
the image of death, and there are many other images
in other cultures and many other species. yes, i attend
other beings. for the beetle, i appear as a beetle,
the appropriate image, then i eat the head; for some trees
i am a fungus that links them to all other trees nearby.

a species of fly emerges from its larval state without
a mouth, and just enough energy to mate. the adult
salmon digests its own body before it mates, the last
indigestible remainder feeds others, the last regrets
evaporate—to them i appear as an explosion."

                                        "what is
the strangest death you witnessed?" the girl asked.
    death answered, "i think the death of equilibrium,
the new understanding that nature is a process pushed
by the pressure of life, continuously to greater
and greater heat and velocity."
    "must i die for some idea of balance?"

                            "what may be best
for you may not help nature or the species. the loss
of an individual—" death paused and took a step back
as she touched his arm again, the continued, "how can
the loss of amphibians make a difference in warsaw?
how can a city change the temperature somewhere
and wipe out a line—death is not loss of harmony,
but part of larger—"

                        "are you nervous?" she smiled,
"are you the death of water also? of air? of forests?"

            "unfortunately, yes, although these things are more
complex. to them i appear as a void—and now
we must disappear."

picnic at swan point

i was sitting by the stone angel, looking over
the small hills of stones carved with comforting phrases:
'he's found eternal rest,' 'she rests in heaven now,'
'he's gone to a better place.' one tombstone read:
'not dead, only sleeping,' and no alarm will ever wake
him either, i thought, an oddly appropriate sentiment
in a cemetery, which meant in greek, to put to sleep.
put to sleep by the kiss of death, i laughed, not
the phone call of death, or the handshake of death, but
then my phone rang and as i lifted it to my lips
i saw a cloud form over a gravestone with a winged angel,
winged death and through the apparition i could read
the carved words momento mori (remember dying).
the form reached out a hand, which i ignored.

"time for the diet of worms?" i spoke into the phone.
          "if you wish," the form answered.
"no i prefer coyotes to worry the bones."
          "not your worry now," he whispered.

death, the final diet

"dead, the word is germanic in origin, is it not, meaning mortal?
does die come from diet?"

                         "no," answered death, "diet is just
a way of life."

                 "well, i'll finally be on a diet, now," art chuckled.
"it isn't just about the purity of bones," death said seriously.
"you must have sinew and skin and even fat; it is form."

         art faced his tormentor and said, "look, i'm just
overweight, certainly you can ignore me today? i've got
a meeting! i can't face death now!"

                 but death ignored him and continued:
"facing death or defacing death it doesn't matter as
the face-off permits the skull to remain. time to go—food
is not a concern now, nor is that business meeting. come."

  "wait, i need to have my body preserved."

                            "to keep it
from the circuits of recycling?"

                   "no, to be there for me at
the end of time."

           "it wouldn't be there, and it would interrupt
the play of eater and eaten, for surely we are eaten,
if not by wolves, then by worms. time to enter the play."

death has a crisis

"you are evil, god is the supreme good," the very large
woman said.

death shrugged and answered: "no, even god
does not believe that, she knows she can not do everything
she wants or she would be as bad a villain as you
would make me."

"i cannot die, my soul will live on."
"you are denying death. nice try. the soul is not a crop
harvested by perfect good," and death passed through her.

what does it mean to help people to die? death asked himself.
is that it? do they appreciate it? care? do they want to know
beforehand? should he just shut up, take them, or continue
to speak with them, make them understand he cared
that his touch was the last they would feel and so
much more meaningful for that? no. what can he do then?
how could he leave his mark on the planet? find meaning
in his own existence?

"after the first, there is no other death," he said, the little
writer with the crooked bowtie.

"no," said death himself,
"every death is first for the subject, and let us not lose sight
of the individual whose universe is scattering." and death
withdrew him.

death needed a special meaning, not as one of two
contrasting fictions: the romantic harvester or the brutal
destroyer of beauty and promise. no, he needed
a middle way.

death practices joking

is the reaper always grim? no. must he be ever serious?
no, he could joke, show people how to laugh at death, make
the reality less solemn but, first he needed to practice,
tell a few stories, relax the clients but, how? what was funny
about shuffling off the mortal coil? banana peels? too crude
too physical. he could think up a good joke to tell
so that laughter would be the last sound and a smile
the last expression they knew. he considered:
'life is a terminal disease' (he had seen the bumper sticker).
he could make up a joke: how many angels could fit
on the head of a pin? depended on the wingspan—
no that wasn't it. where did the idea for fountains come from:
vomiting. why are peoples heads round: the ball inside rolls
longer. this was not going to work. he had to forget
the jokes. maybe for now he would just use their names
to appear more relaxed and friendly.

always leave 'em laughing? smiling?   content?

death gets personal

death names amber
"amber, i'm here," death coolly intoned like a matinee idol
he remembered taking once.
                              "i'm young, i know nothing
of death," the young girl said, as death looked around
her room at the posters of the dead kennedys, comic book
skeletal villains—death images everywhere, but unreal
beings sanitized of real feelings; her parents had tried
to spare her any brush with death or unpleasantness
from living but that was pride, they should have taught her
the skill of mortality, the exchange of gifts, the gifts of life
and death. he smiled and gave her a gift.

and willi
"did i fail to live to my ideal?" the hopi boy asked. "did
i have bad thoughts of the dead? are you an alus
ghost?"
          "no, you are not two-hearted." death assured the boy.
"was it a witch? are you a witch?"
                              "yes," death answered.
"i am a repentant witch and i must be a good shaman
or i will die myself." death knew this would please
the boy as they ghosted away.

kisho
"death is inevitable, the loss of everything dear
is unavoidable." kisho said.
                    and death relaxed.
"is this punishment for my mother?"
                              "what do you think?"
death asked, unrelaxing, knowing the mother had threatened
her death to admonish kisho as a child, and he would believe
as he would.
                    kisho bent slightly, "to the inevitable."

santosa
"ah, the adjal," said santosa.
                              "yes, i have arrived, but it is not
a predestined hour, nothing is really predestined—"
"my death!"
                    "yes, but not the time," death said, looking around
the indonesian town, at the changes. "think of me as a 'talkin,'
the death whisperer of instructions."
                                    "what do i do?"
"nothing, no one really needs help, the process is easy.
there are no proper answers to the angel of death. your soul
has expressed its desires in dreams, so think of this
as a dream, but you will not want to wake."
                                        "ah, i am ready
then."

bhudev
the helper woke in the morning and announced he was going
to die, but would write a poem before that event. then
bhudev laid down his pen, called death and i came.
                                        "i welcome you,
death, i have been prepared since i was thirteen.
i am acquainted with nonbeing. it is the same as before
i was born. i wonder if i helped many—"
    "tsk, tsk," i said, "the only answer to some questions is:
don't ask, especially if you know the answer or that there
is no answer."
                        "i have chanted your name until i am living my
life in shin-jin."
                        "well, you are right about not coming back,
even as a grasshopper," i said.
                                "as long as it is right now."
bhudev replied.

hjordis

"think of death as a teacher" death suggested.

"yea, a dumb teacher, that tells not the student what he needs to know." the scientist answered from his bed.

"perhaps the lesson simply was not observed by you before it applied to you," death offered, "you never saw a songbird fall? your kitty cat get squished, leaves, relatives lie still? notice the thread breaking?"

"why wasn't i told?"

"why would you have to be? isn't it obvious? besides, being dumb means not speaking,"

"no, i wasn't," hjordis noted, "everyone screamed immortality, extension, new scientific fixes."

"death is the only teacher at this level and here no information passes to you, but that doesn't mean it does not pass to the bacteria. your learning should have been on the living side. here is lesson 'n.'"

kapera

"so you are an editor?" death noted, "i am kind of an editor too, but i always say no, no more—or end!"

"but, you're not the creator."

"no, but creation would stop without my work. think about it. if every yes were allowed to live, it would fill existence with mediocrity— i eliminate all eventually but certainly the unfit and dull immediately. imagine steven king without an editor."

"bad example."

"oh, yes, right."

"immediately? i suspect not, have you looked at our civilized gene pool lately? dullness triumphant."

"do you know what your name means?"
"yes, 'will die,' every name has a similar silent vowel."
"after you," death motioned politely.

lien

"your trouble," the candidate assessed his taker—
and death was the taker, not the maker—
"is that you areoneirotaxic."

                "oh, please," death answered,
"i never confuse fantasy and reality. i know them both
as one. you must be onomatomanic, preoccupied
with names and words, and let it not be said that death is so
easily undone. now come."
               "i want to be the one who escapes,
who continues as long as he likes," the librarian answered.

   "but, why?" death asked, "you will never be ready, no matter
how long the extra time. now, exhale and check out. the fine
for overdue— ha, ha, ha, sorry it just seemed so funny—"
   "no, laughing becomes you, let's go then, the split is made."

death meets his match

"epictetus said: 'death does not concern me.
when i am here, he is not'—"
              "A slight overlap, if you want—"
death paused.
           "i don't!" veren exclaimed, "maybe—"
and death nodded, the last of the day, before a rest.
veren continued: "have you ever eaten human flesh?"
   "i don't eat," death said unnecessarily.
                 "i have. near
the casuarina coast with the 'people.' it was either that
or become an edible."
         i hate taking anthropologists, death
thought
     "i know it is not about control, but its lack,"
veren said, "although you can practice the art of dying,
so popular in spain at one time with the pestilence and war
of the 1400s. puppets were popular then, like this wolf
puppet here," and veren pointed to the top of his television
set. "what do you feel?" veren asked suddenly.
   "understanding, respect," death answered.
               "for me?" veren

gawped, "certainly not."

"for the process, the matrix,"
death mused, remembering.

"is this a wild death or a tame
one, mediated by love?"

"death is always wild," death said.
"how can you feel, you're not real, like a dream."

"you're are closer than you know. a dream is
the mind's way of integrating the day; and makes it
meaningful; in that way, i help you understand and summarize
your life."

"so you're like a brain function?"

"i am independent
of each brain, think of me as a spirit shared by all living
beings."

"like a god?"

"no, i have no powers, to save or
change you."

"can you connect me with my wife?" veren asked.
"no, that connection died, but i can tell you she was not
worried about you, only michael."

"michael, yes, i understand,
generations always take the opposite road. is he——?"

"i can tell you he is not dead."

"thank you."
death asked, "what is your secret name?"

"i will not speak it," veren said, "it took too long to find
and tame it——it is the name of a dead man of course.
someday someone else will find mine and use it.
thus the dead live on in name. do you have such a name?"

"only what i call myself, and no, i will not tell."
"will you explain what is happening to me as it happens?"

"regrettably, i cannot. it is ineffable. do you have any
last words?"

"yes, even if there is no one to hear them:
the man is dead, long live the child."

about the author, violet
reason, obviously a name used
to protect a reputation earned in a
different field of activity in the mainstream
of the unstoppable machine—anything else you
need to know about her can be found through her writings.

The Naked Lena (1994)

reason

Colophon

(suggested by Christopher Morley after the Ionian City
of that name, whose cavalry always concluded
an engagement with a furious charge)

This charge is set in Gill sans
using indesign
on a Macintosh ibook
in the coastal village of Cortez
near a cedar hammock
in the southeast coastal plain
during a late hot spring
between panther surveys

Make-up art by Merissa dePasse:
Man in a Silver Dance Costume, Dancing Shoes, Lupines with Black
Raspberries, Flowers

Make-up art by A.M. Caratheodory & Merissa dePasse:
Apples & Plum, Falling Angels, Still Life: The Artist's Dirty Clothes

Make-up art by A.M. Caratheodory:
The Naked Lena

Book and Cover design by Rian Garcia Calusa
Printing and assistance by Booksurge

www.ingramcontent.com/pod-product-compliance
Lightning Source LLC
Chambersburg PA
CBHW050904120626
46554CB00003B/1003